THE MAN ON THE TRAIN

MATTHEW ALLCOCK

Michael Terence
Publishing

First published in paperback by
Michael Terence Publishing in 2017
www.mtp.agency

www.matthewallcock.com

ISBN 978-1-521-47013-8

For Mary

THE MAN ON THE TRAIN

MATTHEW ALLCOCK

Ours was the marsh country, down by the river, within, as the river wound, twenty miles of the sea.

Charles Dickens. *Great Expectations.*

"There were desperate days when the sand we sifted held no meaning," he said.

"I looked at the plain glass window and saw nothing but reflection, the image of a man absorbed by nothing but his own self."

Across the flat, sweeping expanse of the salty marshes, an image of incomplete exactitude did appear. But its vibrancy and coherence were distorted by the dirty smears that rippled out from a single, fragmented crack in the window-pane as much as by the flickering landscape beyond. The fields bore swathes of inquisitive animals perched atop grassy knolls and gently insinuating streams which broached the spongy terrain with effortless perseverance. Through the crack, it seemed as if the wind could whistle in to speak of untold secrets from faraway lands, that the sun could forge its golden rays into a single, elusive unity.

I stood at a distance, tentatively pawing the still and sultry air that lingered in the train carriage. I had been peremptorily halted by the man's passing thoughts, the substance of which had come to me clearly and without hesitation. In fact, when I stated, "he said", a moment ago, perhaps I was being unclear, disingenuous maybe. And I'll have you know, I am nothing if not clear.

What I should say, rather, is "he thought". For these articulations were born in a quite different way to the mild utterances of speech or the harsh declamations of authority that go to comprise "spoken" language. Nor were these articulations simply bodily gestures, inferred on my part from physical movements or subconscious tics. Rather, these messages, if I am able to call them that, came to me not as expected or solicited responses, nor readily anticipated or scalable sounds; no, instead, they came more like great, directionless tsunamis, torrential in their impact and stunning in their implication. For, I should state unequivocally now, that I possess the ability to have unrivalled access to people's thoughts, that I wander the carriages of trains, that I am a spectre, a fraction of my former self.

If I am to ride the wave, so to speak, of these undiscriminating outbursts, I have necessarily to install a kind of filtering system. This has come to me over the months. From the early days of emotional disorientation and mental collapse when I was bombarded by a hail of unforeseen leave-takings, unwarranted eruptions, and unthinking recriminations, I have since learnt to separate out all but the most pertinent remarks, a task that has been as exhausting as it has been worthwhile.

Right now, these approaches are nothing unusual to me. For I have become accustomed to the regular assaults on consciousness that fail to administer notice of their impulsive arrival, adapting much like an hotelier who finds one day that his guest has departed without so much as a note of goodbye or a token of thanks. You learn to adjust, to make do, and to press on. I myself have become used to apprehending the passing reflections and momentary reminiscences of the innocent train passengers, finding in them something solid and substantial where before there was only haze and ambiguity.

It is almost as if I am able to capture that transient kernel of truth from the depths of a person's imagination and memory, that I have access to hidden zones of meaning denied everyone else. You'll testify to this experience, I know. You'll testify to that frustrating and nauseating incapacity borne by all but the most gifted of individuals, that inability to retain or arrest those thoughts and ideas that nevertheless imprint an indelible note of profundity on the soul. They come so rarely, but these moments are marked by a gentle lift, a surge of life and happiness that dissolves the surrounding gloom in an eruption that sends out ripples in all directions, circumscribing all and sundry, and impacting upon everyone.

Perhaps these moments only come at night, when the barriers to self-realisation or, should I say, the barriers that fortify the self in all its apartness and isolation, crumble to the ground like sandcastles lying too close to the water's edge, broken by a crisp wave in the early summer dawn. If you recognise this understanding, however tentatively, you'll reckon my skill here somewhat enviable. Yet you'd be mistaken. I've lost something I can never recover and I've only recently come to know it.

For I roam this predetermined space now. Some might say I'm a fugitive, an absentee on the run from truth. Either way, I float along forlornly, touching no one, invisible to the naked eye, contemptuous of nothing but myself. What brought me here was the comforting security of it all, the way the physical train-carriage represents a space of familiar certainty that opposes the wandering thoughts and reflections of the railway passengers which, released from the shackles of human finitude, can traverse diverse and unique landscapes without limit or encumbrance. The way the train hugs the tracks with unswerving dedication, ripping the air and disturbing the grassy verges with regular and unbiased emphasis.

When the right person comes along with

some new perspective that can shed light on my own past, I am able to burrow deeper into my subjectivity, to get closer to that something that I've let slip. After having met a few of these so-called important figures who have allowed me the opportunity to piece together how I got into this state in the first place, what they've said, or what I've overheard them think, has triggered something deep down in my unconscious, something hidden from view by a protective mechanism, a defensive barrier.

The man in the brown overcoat whose thoughts had involuntarily entered my stream of consciousness appeared strangely familiar, more so than the other figures who broached my headspace that day. With his face turned then towards the land, then towards the sea, he met my pensive gaze only on occasion, fighting a furrowed brow with the urge to appear amiable.

As for me, I take a train ride every day, pacing solemnly at a given hour and in a given space, rightly fulfilling my duty by forgoing the air. At times, I feel myself to be awfully numb, as if my mind is subconsciously safeguarding some notion of freedom that refuses examination. At others, I find that I am suspended in harmless satisfaction in the old world, invisible to others as much as to the wind that gently and unfathomably goads my skin. It is becoming clearer now though, this state of living. If I return to the beginning, maybe I can show you how.

It's been said before that one of the most important questions one can pose to a fellow human being is that which enquires into their first remembered experience. That memory which is mined from the depths of one's mind, plundered from obscurity and chiselled and moulded into something definitive and precious, is seen to be somehow meaningful against your character - it places you in a context from which one can evaluate what in the world you most value, how you see yourself, and what this says in terms of the rest of your past life.

But its purpose is just as significant in relation to the human power to remember. When do people become so aware of themselves that they are able to store up memories for later inspection, and is this a conscious process or in any way traceable? At what point does a person know that they are them and not another, and where exactly do the boundaries lie between the self and the external world? And is this point in time ever identifiable with any degree of certainty – an entrenched or unalterable determinant of your future life?

These questions - ones which delve into

fundamental notions of human identity - are difficulties that I have turned over agonisingly (sometimes savouring them, more often than not dismayed by them), during my months spent in the train carriage. The reason they have assumed such importance in my mind is down to the very personal and singular experience I've had of witnessing a kind of new birth, the opportunity I've been gifted for a second chance. It needn't be emphasised, therefore, that, despite the ability I have to reappraise those first fledgeling moments of consciousness where I found myself thrown into a completely new kind of existence, my attempt to describe such an experience in words is problematic and often futile.

Yet I endeavour to provide the reader with all the information I've gleaned from my time here, in an attempt to acknowledge and understand. No matter how imperfect words are as a vehicle for my message, this account serves as legitimacy for all that I've lived.

My first recollection is of a train announcement formed of unidentifiable sounds. What the exact nature of this address was I cannot possibly say. Perhaps it was something along the lines of "This Train is the service to L- V-., calling at ...", a phrase that I have come to be familiar with over the months, repeated as it is frequently and with unimpeachable devotion. Perhaps it was an intimate conversation travelling illicitly and fearlessly across the airwaves or a ticket inspector kindly asking someone to pay the fare. Or perhaps it was a mixture of these things, a complex combination of man-made and artificial resonances, a hybrid of elemental and compound sounds.

This matter is destined to remain in abeyance in spite of the time spent speculating upon it. All I can say with any certainty is that sound of some sort bounced about my eardrums, ricocheting as if within a pinball machine. It was inescapable and unforgiving, forcing its way inexorably through my body, triggering other senses as a toppled domino would the rest of the pack. The notion I had was one of holistic, integrated being – a situation where all sensual impulses responded and adhered to one another.

Inside the ecstasy, the air pounded about my skin, pressing from innumerable, directionless points. I found my perception aligning itself with darting scenes of unimaginable complexity, building cumulatively, layer upon layer. Sights swarmed in a series of grids and blotches; smells coincided with blurts of noise; and synapses fired to forewarn of prickling sensations about the toes and ears. Unable to situate myself or contest my surroundings, something gripped at my midriff and refused to let go.

I write from the point of view of someone attempting to recover himself. This is what I heard.

The doors on the carriage closed like pincers, splicing the air in twain. The electronics on the display board registered as meaningless dots and indecipherable fragments, only gradually assuming some form of coherence as they tallied with the speaker overhead, propounding the train's movements in a cold and eerie way. And people milled about me with a speed that was neither fast nor slow, but somehow both.

Vainly striving to temper the commotion, my mind responded in ways I couldn't begin to understand. I'd been coerced by a bristling, primal power, exposed to the light, the sound, the vacancy of the carriage. It was as if I'd confronted the underlying chaos of existence - that basic dialogue between fusion and diffusion that underwrites the idea of creation. It felt as if I was closer to things in their actual state of smashing intensity. At the same time, however, I was savagely tired and remote, yet somehow more keenly aware than I could ever be.

On top of this, nothing had context. One stroke of discomfort was quickly replaced by another, totally removed from its former frame of reference and unrecognisable as an emotion with familiar episodes and progressions. I felt myself repeatedly questioning my situation, unable to settle on any angle with conviction, unsure of my opinion even when it came to matters of pressing urgency. The colour of the carriage, the presence of the sound, the nature of my body – all had to be revised and reconsidered. Anything less seemed an abnegation of the truth.

The task at hand was to somehow grasp where I was, who I was, what I was. With no immediate memory of my past, I was unidentifiable, not just to others but to myself. I experienced the lightness of simple feeling - pure, unmediated, blessed being. Like an animal thrust into the world's frenzy, I was pure matter, comprising drives and instincts, pressures and revulsions. Yet I possessed a semblance of self-awareness, a willingness to investigate my role in relation to the environment, a deep-down urge to piece together meaning, to learn about value, to explain and understand.

But I was invisible, unheard, untouched. No one responded to my advances. I invited dialogue and contact, quietly and tentatively at first, then passionately, some might say desperately. I entreated passengers to display some recognition of my existence, pleading with them to offer assistance so that I could, in turn, help them. But they all met my stare vacantly, barely acknowledging even the faint fluctuations in air pressure my bodily presence must have incurred.

I quickly sensed the low-down throb of acute isolation; an ache so searing, so prevalent and nauseous, that it crippled me in a physical heap. The thought of being unnoticeable and unaccountable had impressed itself sharply on me for a moment, thrilling me with its limitless, and as yet unexamined, potential. But my enthusiasm for the latent possibility of my predicament passed rather quickly. The anxious excitement I initially felt was curiously unsatisfying and nothing if not fleeting.

Indeed, my pleasure was stymied somewhat by the harsh revelation that all efforts at broaching the materiality of the carriage were fruitless and in vain. It appeared the usual physical laws that govern the order of things were applicable to me just as much as to anyone else.

That I could hardly feel my limbs tumble down upon the carpeted floor of the carriage nonetheless removed nothing from the notion of an altogether frightful understanding. It was almost as though I could taste the fear, smell the animosity, clutch the desperation.

Anxiety pervaded its way up through my torso, emanating from a nucleus that was at once unlocatable and incontestable. And then, out of the cacophony of noise that assaulted my headspace, silence: nothing but a low-frequency hum with regular tremors and an asinine buzz that should have been beyond the range of human hearing.

As I recall the heartache and terror of those early moments, my mind fails to find the words to do justice to the experience. I'd woken up to a modern day version of hell, realising that I couldn't talk, couldn't associate, couldn't be free with other people. That I was alone and totally vulnerable to forces outside of my control added to the weight of my isolation.

Yet I still possessed the vocabulary and the power to think in basic terms, the means of conceptualising my environment through language. It was as if I'd retained - from wherever I'd come from - much of the knowledge and many of the skills I'd hitherto possessed. What had disappeared, however, was my past, my memory and history - the ways in which one forms an identity on a day-to-day basis.

In short, I was destitute and homeless, perhaps mad. That the mythical ideal of invincibility and superhuman capacity was denied in this realm too - or so I thought at the time - was curiously saddening. Having yet to be tutored in the full scope of my abilities - for instance, my gift for having access to other people's thoughts - I remained rather innocent and naïve for a long while. Even so, when looking back on my attitude then, I appraise it with a kind of nostalgic regret, a strange sadness that laments the loss of a simpler time when the full complexity of the world had yet to be revealed.

Before I'd become aware of this ability to listen to the internal dialogue of the strangely distant train passengers, I frantically strove to escape the cacophony of my immediate situation, scurrying away from the people snugly cooped up in their seats into the connecting chamber between carriages.

After breaking away into this restful limbo which provided momentary solace and a kind of temporary peace, I all at once began to assume the most lucid and transparent vision of the landscape surrounding the train. This is the fiercest impression I've retained, the most indelible and timeless. It's stuck to me with more certainty than the fleeting and sharp-angled impressions I surmised at the beginning of the experience – a fact which may be attested to in the struggle to describe such an occurrence in words. My mind settled immediately and conclusively on the flat, broad marshland that enfolded the train tracks on either side, finding in it something universal and maternal, something homely.

I contemplated the terrain with dreamy awe, feeling a creeping and irrepressible urge to shuffle closer to it, to touch it and know it completely. My hands wandered up eagerly against the glass panels of the double-doors, clutching the febrile air before it dissolved away in mute nothingness. The coolness of its touch coloured my vision. The marshes looked like a feathery sponge, spotted with salty grains and ruffled with luscious heather. Circular pools of icy looking water shivered lightly as the wind spread its wispy tongue over their surface, lapping up invisible flecks of condensation to feed back into the atmosphere and resume matter's natural cycle. Pockets of roaming animals stood still next to ditches, arching their necks at the whistling train, punctuating their observations to gather the next mouthful of food or survey the whereabouts of their offspring several strides away. And the weak, winter sky seemed to bear heavily down upon them.

Inside the carriage, I breathed steadily in and out, out and in, testing the air's consistency with my hand and marvelling at it as if experiencing it for the first time. Right before me, shiny, white clouds drifted on and on across the heavens, and new and elaborate mist formations appeared ceaselessly over the wooded ground on the horizon.

I enjoyed spending this time suspended in regular motion, watching the water flow in bountiful streams and the animals, faithfully mindless of their lengthening shadows, repeat their hardened tread. The train was great at keeping me on a course which was both straight and narrow. Finding the space in my own mind, I was unburdened of the need to feel anxious or afraid. And I was allowed to spend many further hours in melancholy contemplation of the distant countryside, observing it as we trundled on endlessly.

At empty and imponderable times, I'd like to employ my thoughts in a meditation that amounted to nothing at all, but that captured, in its void transparency, something of the desolate chill of the marshland.

Yet as I studied the environment more and more, I noticed how the dewy surface provided a neat counterpoint to the technological efficiency of the train. Despite the allure of its unpredictability, the marshes provoked just as much fear and foreboding in me as they did awe and wonder. They were evidently governed by irregular forces that obeyed random and chaotic laws. Because of this, I found myself picturing the wild and anarchic land as a series of grids, rigidly aligned and definitively circumscribed, so as to conceptualise it in a reassuringly conclusive manner.

I erected hedges and stone walls in my mind, tending to them whenever they showed signs of deterioration or neglect, evidence that they'd been left to subsist under the auspices of pure chance - blind, inscrutable fate. Before the walls were up, there existed no limits. I'd returned to the swamp before the flux and upheaval of civilised progress, and this scared me. To wit, I found myself building up a map of the marshes, parcelling them up into known and unknown lands so as to be better placed if I were ever to chance across them.

Conversely, the train carriage provided a man-made space that could be, to a much greater extent, patrolled and contained. The mechanical complexity and scientific rationality of the machinery fascinated me from the outset and I took to studying the connections and processes that facilitated its workings as best I could.

Yet something about my deep regard for

how the train carriages came to be formed struck me as strangely uncharacteristic. I assumed it had its roots in the situation I'd found myself in - trapped, isolated and alone. The demand that I become self-sufficient and knowledgeable in the basics of survival meant I took up the study of subjects I'd never been known to appreciate before.

This preoccupation was extremely important to me and captured something integral inside that I shall go on to discuss at greater length later on. It was predicated on a deeply felt lack – the feeling that I was so alienated and unaware of many of the basic processes that go to underwrite existence, the feeling that I could and should do better.

For the time being, I wish to describe the yearning instinct that took hold of me after a short while in the connecting chamber, an urge to find an image of myself, to discover a reflection in a window or a likeness in a mirror; to look directly and unshrinkingly on what I'd become.

I crept furtively through the lightly flapping door of a lavatory cubicle, mindful of the harsh, scraping sound that seemed to filter up accusingly from beneath the train. The air was still, slightly tepid and damp. The light was as bright and artificial as a gold tooth. As I took a moment to adjust my posture, the light seemed to lose its lustre. Right before me stood the full length of a man I'd have to get to know once again from the beginning. Strangely hunched and unshaven around the chin, with piercing blue eyes and a pinched nose, I was incongruously unkempt, caught in the mocking glare of the spotlight above me, a monument to brute unreflection.

The shock of my appearance was manifestly enhanced by the claustrophobic nature of the space, the way the light seemed to bounce around frantically in a desperate attempt at escaping its surroundings. I passed my fingers gently through my beard, scraping it occasionally to get a sense of texture. I blinked indulgently, watching the pools of beady moisture glaze my eyes, appearing and reappearing endlessly. I even took the time to arch my neck and turn away my face, finding tender satisfaction in the play of shadows, the distortions of perspective. Up against the ventilation shaft, a timid moth appeared to be doing the same.

I wasn't alone for long in the bright cubicle, however, woken peremptorily from my contemplative state by a hesitant knock at the lavatory door. For an instant, I'd forgotten my ability to go unseen and reacted in a naturally defensive manner, blurting out that the room was occupied. This being the first attempt I'd made at communication though, I was startled to observe how no words formed in my mouth. Articulate expressions were replaced instead by futile gasps of air, empty and naked, the words ripped from within me as if they'd expired due to lack of use. The stranger outside repeatedly grasped the door handle, but on discovering their exertions to have no avail, appeared to step back and relent.

I wondered how I'd be able to vacate the area without drawing attention to myself, or rather the lack of myself. Waiting anxiously on one side of the divide, I imagined scenarios where I'd be caught out, chained up and put through an arbitrary penance, made to explain myself to others when I'd no understanding of how I'd even come to be there. I envisaged torturous scenes that could only have resided in the depths of my unconscious, formed out of the accumulated ephemera of images and dreams of a past life, the wastes and scrag-ends of real and imagined experience.

The connecting chamber sounded dormant so I made a pass at leaving the cubicle. Not wishing to disturb the peace, I trod ever so lightly, barely troubling the carpeted floor, wary of avoiding preventable distractions. The stranger who I presumed had tried the handle was a man in strangely ill-fitting clothes, his back turned discreetly away from me, his eyes keenly attached to the marshland. From the slightness of his neck and the austere blankness of his fair hair, I envisaged a man with undecided eyes and a melancholic air. His movements were kept to a minimum. Only on occasion did he glance at the flimsy broadsheet newspaper lolling lightly in his hands.

It appeared that I'd been able to escape the cubicle unnoticed and unseen. This was enough for now. To be sure, the man may suspect some misdemeanour, some petty prank. He may suspect neglect or a lack of thought. Or he may question his immediate judgment, adamant that the door was locked and unassailable, but simultaneously unsure of his own certainty.

I had no reason to be needlessly alarmed though, and the prospect of explaining myself or of answering to some higher authority had been deferred at least for now. Rather, I was confronted by the first taste of something completely new.

As I travelled the space between the stranger and myself, I began to piece together opaque words and fleeting sentences, sounds that contained meaning because they were symbolic, sounds that were communicative because they were human. The stranger's thoughts, as I later became more willing to understand, were being relayed to me across the airwaves.

Initially, I experienced a great rush of excitement, the kind of heady, unreal feeling one gets from walking on an unblemished morning. How clearly the words sang to me, I thought, now set free from enslavement and allowed to move openly in the uncluttered air. Removed from discord and disharmony, these reflections were determinate and complete. They were divested of heaviness and struggle, moulded in clean and bright crystals that sparkled with intensity and meaning as surely as spots of moisture on an early morning dew. I spread my hands in a gesture that meant all things were possible, abandoning myself to vivid and unadulterated joy.

Yet my enthusiasm was tempered somewhat by the recognition that I was unable to share in this revelation. I felt the need to pass on my knowledge to the man who'd played such a vital part in its fruition. But his ability to participate was perhaps confirmed by an ignorance of my presence.

As I pieced together his articulations, I found myself uniquely able to capture the substance of his thoughts, expertly adept at retaining them for further rumination, even though I was powerless to touch the man in response. Captured with of a curious mixture of exhilaration and unease, the stranger appeared to shimmer, as if he'd walked straight out of his own story.

"We travelled for what felt like miles across the blue-black sea, fending off fierce waves and lapping tides as they lurched at our heels and over the stern. We'd waited for hours to let the storms clear, feebly eyeing our chartered boat as it bounced passively against the harbour-side. It was the height of summer when the days were longest and the weather the most hospitable. Now, aboard and in motion, we caught our first glimpse of the ancient crags rising up out of the mist - time-honoured rock formations that were as steep as they were wild, a world away from the tidy lawns and privet hedges of our cosy suburban homes.

Flocks of screaming seabirds formed an acrobatic halo over the mountain-top, steadily reclaiming the land that was always theirs to own.

It's said in a number of documents how the former inhabitants of this remote and inaccessible island were forced to evacuate their homes, a result of life-threatening cliff erosion. Certainly, the half-destroyed cottages and weeping rocks are definitive monuments to decay and the tantalising force of nature. According to the textbooks, signs of a lost community abound - an archaeological minefield as one newspaper put it.

To be sure, someone somewhere would be keen to talk us through photographs of that long-forgotten era, eager to reminisce on the spirit of those faces that stare back at you, half-smiling at the lens and the future. But we required first-hand knowledge of the island, unquestionable evidence from the most reliable and honest witness, the land herself. And it really did feel that we'd come far to be here - we really did seem to be hovering on the edge of the world.

A strange mythical allure had possessed the collective imagination of our crew, uniting us in a common aim to explore this sacred place. It served as an emphatic example of what some call a certain "islomania", that rare affliction of the heart which results in a strong attraction to outlying land.

I started to ponder what those final moments were like when the Islanders were finally leaving their home, collected aboard separate vessels, drifting away from everything they'd ever known. I'd heard an old man in a pub once remark how the sea could beat so hard that it would leave the Islanders lip-reading for a week. Trees would not grow and the salty water meant crops had to be carefully placed to avoid instant decimation. Fishing was deemed treacherous and many inhabitants drowned in the turbulent groundswell a few streets offshore.

There was one quality the island didn't lack though: seabirds. Three-quarters of a million of them came every year to nest on the sea stacs: gannets, fulmars, kittiwakes, puffins, great skua, razorbills, guillemots and petrels. The islanders subsisted largely off these birds, ensnaring them in their traps or catching them by suspending on ropes from the cliff-tops.

How people could manage to climb the stacs, I'd never understood. But learning their skills from a young age, both men and women quickly became experts in their chosen field. Little was thrown away: fulmar bones and the bills of oystercatchers made fastenings for clothes, the skin of gannet's necks made shoes. Feathers and fulmar oil went to the Laird to pay the rent.

The seas around the island are renowned for their tidal rips, races and whirlpools. Early settlers believed in ritual appeasements offered to the gods as a vital way of calming the ferocious ocean. Otherwise, they took their measures from the flight of the fowls.

We'd been cautious to consult various journals and experts in the field, and there had been times on our journey when a little prayer did escape from the mouths of a few of us as our sails reefed against a rising wind. As we arrived, however, the sea had calmed, the air was chill, and the sky had assumed a distinctly purple hue.

The top half of the crag before us stuck out of the ocean like a giant blade, appearing crystallised by the corrosive sea. But upon closer inspection, we could make out tens of thousands of gannets sitting on their nests.

The abandoned buildings formed a thin line that stretched into the island's centre: the church and schoolroom, the factor's house, where the laird's representative lived, the post office, then the homes of the other islanders and the hundreds of small storage buildings where inhabitants dried and kept food. In front of them all stood the rectilinear frame of an army base.

Since the evacuation, the only year-round residents had been military personnel at the radar station, built fifty years before as part of a missile range. The buildings were largely boarded up and closed off about the door with grills. Through the dust, one could barely make out the names of past families: Gillies, MacDonald, McGregor. I tried to imagine what it would have been like on a busy market day with small boats in the bay, women fetching the groceries, and children tending to the cows. The innocence, purity, simplicity and freedom of that way of life struck me deeply. With increasing contact with the outside world, however, many young men left to earn a living in the cities on the mainland and farms began to be deserted, left untended and unloved.

Their way of life was never the same again. Not used to money and the many idiosyncrasies of the air in the towns, many ex-islanders struggled with disease, both physical and mental.

But for many, a broadening of horizons did take place and adaptation to new surroundings was possible. In fact, the majority deem the present conclusively better than the past; the new way of life a definite advance on the exhausting and difficult methods of years gone by. And the acceptance has been borne willingly - that the land has been won back by its rightful owners.

Alighted on the island and out of reach of the sticky mosses that blushed the bay, I followed the neglected pathway leading to the island's centre. The dilapidated buildings stood tethered to the ground, trembling in their humble way like frozen fists before the clutches of time.

The whole area was overawed by one indomitable peak that poked its silhouetted head up above the clouds. With thunderous majesty, it simultaneously invited and dismissed approach. To venture to the top of the mountain and look down upon the griddled floor; to cast my sight back through history and join a cast of millions; to contemplate the sweeping terrain as it merged into wilderness – this has always been my wont. Wherever I travel in the world, I always look for something to climb. Even if it is only to rush back down the incline in a blaze of breathless motion, the need to enter another world far from absolutely everything never fails to grip me like a fever.

As I laboured on with head bent earthward as if in opposition to an enemy, everything seemed to run at me through the mist. Patches of greenery blinked through the haze and strobes of light made blotchy and uncertain impressions on my eager mind.

Locations were indistinct and grew less present as I began scaling upwards, clawing vigorously at purplish bracken and stomping mindlessly over the moistened heather.

The clouds scurried across the sky at an alarming rate as the wind picked up its full force and the weather changed. And if the likelihood of achieving a decent view from the peak seemed highly dubious; if at several points, I'd assumed I'd haplessly lost my way or become aware of the insignificance of my lowly self, then the general urge to climb higher, to achieve greater perspective and more visible authority, rallied me on with greater and greater fervour, like an intoxicating, inexhaustible tonic.

Cloying nervousness became chirpy enthusiasm and a bird leapt up above the puffy clouds. No trees graced the stubborn upper slopes of the peak and shrubbery contended diligently but failingly with the merciless weather. Today was evidently calmer than most but the general impression of struggle and strife imbued every organism.

Mercifully, the clouds appeared eager to clear, opening up as if in ceremony to let the light spill out over the coast like a liquid that could reach every pore. I sensed fleeting tremors of exaltation simmer through me, sensations that were peremptorily erased by the belting wind which sought to moderate my misplaced pride.

Yet undiscouraged and breathless, I relinquished commerce with my inner thoughts: there before me, recovered from the plume of mist so recently a defining feature of the sky, stood a building made out of stone, crumbling wearily at the edges, laid out before the pristine serenity and vastness of the land."

I'd been attentive till the man had finished. Softened by the flood of his own thoughts, the usual channels of expression were too narrow for his purpose. Giving a clearer insight into his soul than any formulated expression of words could ever do, he spoke from inside, out of the peace of his surroundings, remaining throughout in silence, standing on stems of stillness that stroke the dim light.

This confrontation with nature, both literally in the form of the marshland and metaphorically in the way of the man's story, had awoken within me something mysteriously hidden. Indeed, it has only been with recollection that the starkness of the revelation has become apparent – namely, that I had been, up until that point, so incontestably immune to all living things, so callously unconcerned by sensual impulses and how impossibly they fill up our every moment.

To touch the stiff, cold, hard legs of a table or to run firmly across the carpeted floor; to sense the vibrancy of the primary colour scheme on a woman's dress or to identify the ineluctable fragrance of a soap bar from the washroom or on one's hands – these are some of the things that have affected me most deeply during my time spent in the train carriage.

When the trees arch out from the mossy

verges lining the tracks, it matters not if they seem repelled by some unknown or unsolicited advance; if the wind turbines that line the horizon and bracket the coast assume the form of a barrier to pass, worry not; for we travel in a green grass of tunnel, across the marshland where the birds huddle closely before their long journey south; where the cows stand stock still and possess the days; where we crouch below an inverted, immutable and boundlessly blue sea, musing endlessly.

For what seemed like days, I'd indulge these frequent excursions into the minds of others, gazing through unseen windows as if viewing other worlds. Twisting galaxies rolled majestically against a backdrop of what looked like dark truth, dotted here and there with oddly knowing stars.

It was only with a focused and determined effort that I fought off the advances of some - their competing claims to be heard and understood - and learnt to absorb only the stories that seemed most compelling to me.

I'd managed to stifle and contain the successive blows as they came, using a technique whereby I'd parcel out words and phrases according to theme. I'd unload them from a kind of memory palace composed of a number of rooms, juggling more and more visitors each day.

Those same terrors that had made me cry out with mercy and confusion in the early moments were now simply hurdles to overcome. With the right agility and strength of training, I was able to adapt to these obstacles as if they were enforced necessities - little inconveniences that one learns to deal with as part of the many unavoidable hardships in the world.

Before long, the whole process became as natural as the intake of air. And on route, the notion came to me more forcefully than ever: we are all mind animals - we spend equally as much time abstracted inside our heads as we do engaging with things around us.

My ability to reign in others and allow them access to my tribulations, however, was significantly diminished as has already been shown. Invisible and mute, I identified with the figures that passed through the train carriage, those that hopped off at the next station and those in for the long haul. But my entreaties were not reciprocated, and for that reason I cannot be said to have been completely content inside.

Who is to say what processes and dialogues came to form my inner being over those weeks; only time will prove how things came to be. And it is not for me to pre-empt or anticipate unduly what I would later learn in quite the unexpected and sudden manner that I did. My first ally was one of many. And if he moved on and learnt to think in different ways, so did I. So that experience can never be said to be static; that if contexts are forever changing, so are our identities; that if I loved myself one day, the same could not be said for the next; that if the air spoke of clarity and freshness for a moment, the skies were soon overtaken by shadows.

Still, for a long time my supple, impressionable mind hungered after insight. I was an empty vessel, launching at the smallest scraps, attaching particular importance to the slightest of words.

Yet if the freedom had been hard won, it wasn't for a lack of effort on my part. My methods of containing the thoughts of the train passengers were unclear from the start. Even I'd look on in awe at my ability to possess and retain, things becoming less and less complicated with the days.

Interrupted only on occasion by a nagging echo of my remoteness, what I didn't recognise then, I do now. Looking back with fresh eyes, I can only review with sympathy and forgiveness how misguided and lost I really was.

My love of trains was nevertheless greatly enhanced over those first few intrepid months. In my role as master of my own universe, I allocated equal time to studying the nature of the world in which I walked as I did to the pragmatic handling of passengers' thoughts. Wowed by the train's incredible display of power and ingenuity and the human creativity that went into composing it, I picked up on things I'd never noticed before, watching it closely as it travelled through the vast open space and across the fertile marshland.

The tracks helped me to delimit this immensity. Crisscrossing the countryside in neat and purposeful strokes, the lines worked in tandem to allow for the easy passing of carriages from one to the next. The solid, iron wheels that skirted the low-friction surfaces moved with awe-inspiring frequency, pumped along by pistons that fired and fired. The whole system was orchestrated to run with dogged efficiency, timetables marking out when and where each vehicle would be, and railway junctions and signalling systems aligned to determine their wishes. And the train itself appeared to glide along effortlessly, the tracks so designed to permit the natural transference of weight to the loose-stoned ground below.

Consisting of two parallel steel rails set at a fixed distance apart, the rails themselves connect to each other by bolted-down railroad ties or sleepers. Set into the loose gravel or ballast, the concrete ties float somewhat off the floor, the weight of the tracks keeping them stabilised.

At times, the notion of weightlessness and freedom amid all this material presence struck me with such force that it felt as if the train were lifting up off the ground, much as an aeroplane would, but not for its own sake.

When rail workers are laying train tracks, the time and effort needed to build and maintain the lines are belied by this feeling, this ease of use. With so little to trouble oneself with on a train as it passes from one station to the next, you resting in your chair with one arm slung casually against the window, your fellow passengers lost in random distraction and thought, is it a wonder that we care little for the energy and vision that has, for centuries, gone into their careful and deliberate constitution? Do we only get to pass judgment on such feats of human imagination when things go wrong or when we have the cause to pause and reflect? Will we ever learn to make the time to value things that have been forgotten through history with more frequency than we currently do? And is this even possible when, in consequence of the film of familiarity and selfish absorption, we struggle to see, hear, or even understand the beauty around us?

The rail has a wide base or foot, a narrow web and a head (wider than the web, but not as wide as the foot). The weights of the rails vary from 80 to 160 pounds (36 to 73 kilogrammes) per yard depending upon the type of train operating on the tracks and the country. Segments of rail track may connect to one another by bolted plates called fishplates, but most modern rail segments are welded together to provide a smooth ride. Steel tracks can be straight or curved to steer the train since steel is easily bent into shape.

Depending upon the topography, some curves may be slightly angled or banked to help the train stay on the track as it negotiates the curve. In many cases, railroad tracks are elevated above the surrounding ground and have drainage systems to remove water. They may also be surrounded by fences to prevent animals and people from wandering on to the tracks. Electrical trains will have either a third power rail or overhanging wires that supply the electricity, deliberately out of reach of those unfortunate enough not to know the hazards for themselves.

As I accumulated more and more knowledge and amassed more and more information, I found myself sensing a deeper connection with the environment around me, rediscovering a certain stirring of life.

Indeed, I appeared to have a rare gift for it; for learning effortlessly and forgetting nothing; for watching everything fall into place on its own. For I'd always felt a tangible disconnect between my own mind and what it had to contend with in the everyday world. The experience of the train carriage served to help me through this. And if on occasion I stumbled or hesitated over my own ability to understand, the support and devotion of the train acted to shore me up. So that if perchance I appeared to wheeze out in exhaustion, hamstrung by my own ineptitude and stunted by the insubstantiality of my thoughts, so did the train wheeze out; that if I hummed and pottered with uncertainty, it did that too; that if I was a physical and finite being in an infinite and frequently witless universe, so too was everything around me.

When we reached the major stations where train tracks converge in a soup of intermingling cables and lines, I'd think of the station wardens exchanging messages on their handheld radios, sensitive to the fact that I was cut off from their hushed and purposeful voice. I imagined the exchanges travelling susceptibly through the air, passed on by invisible networks that flooded the sky, linking up only to dissolve in empty secrecy moments later.

I'd try to absorb these circuits, clenching and releasing my hands in a motion that resembled the pulse of electrical signals. Perhaps in a vain attempt at insinuating my way into the general flow of dialogue around me, I clasped at any means I could muster. But the thought that these currents could melt like raindrops, spilling out over the earth to leave ne'er a trace, struck me with a delicacy I'd never quite experienced before.

Something about the intangibility of it all, the inconsequentiality, the sheer bravado, perhaps, of waves that swarmed around us but that never settled; currents that immersed us in a field of daily interconnection, and yet that showed a willingness to escape, to be transitory and fleeting, as if to stay too long was somehow a violation of their calling. To be sure, this notion was distressing for me, and I was sure to forgo ever mining too deep into such endless mysteries.

In the station waiting rooms and coffee shops, people sat reading newspapers or glancing into space, contemplating their journey ahead by staring at electronic timetables, forming route maps and station names in their minds.

Whenever the train passed through

stations at a certain hour of the day, the sun was at a height so that visibility into these rooms was hard to non-existent. The foggy glare against the cold window panes sent a blaze of obscurity across the top half of the rooms and the ceiling, shedding people of their upper layers and abandoning them to disembodied motion from the waist down. I'd imagine the remainder of these figures as they propped themselves up against wooden table shelves, human asides on the lusciously fuzzy horizon.

The stories I fashioned out of these momentary transitions were fired by the names of provincial train stations – Whitstable, Teynham, Faversham, Newington - providing me with material to elaborate entire worlds. For, with such a dearth of natural interaction available, I found myself relying more and more on the sporadic imaginings and gentle artifice of my own mind.

As we approached the city for the first time and left the marshlands behind, gradually becoming scooped up in a sea of twinkling house lights and steaming motorways that resembled long rifts of tar, I mentally adjusted to make allowances for an altogether different scenery. The train would become busier as it approached its terminus and at hours of particular popularity I'd squeeze in between people and observe their vacant stares. Brushing up against a man's neck or lolling beside the cautious dress of a lady would send a shimmer of excitement through me, suggestive of the way barriers can be bridged, however precariously.

I began to see myself less as a separate and self-contained person, less a consequential and independent individual, and more a part of a greater whole, a whole that wasn't aware of its mutuality, but that nonetheless existed somewhere, somehow.

I'd miss the marshes and think that next time I'd venture out onto their salty terrain. But the opportunity to observe the flow and motion of city folk in their breathless ways was a pleasure to me, a way of punctuating the incessant emptiness of the marshland where not a single figure wandered for no one dwelt there.

Enclosed in their own little bubbles, mindfully disregarding of one another, the workers formed a troupe of by-and-large indistinguishable individuals. The way they adopted the routines and mannerisms offered to them by convention seemed to jar with their haughty complacency and self-assurance. It was as if their actions were theirs to own, theirs to label, theirs to live out entirely and possess. Standing apart in opposition, they appeared fully in touch, fully purposeful, and yet strangely mute and without direction, wrongly thinking they'd chosen their life when in fact it had chosen them.

Still, the regularity of their arrival - the sheer assumption I was able to afford in the cycle day after day - lent my experience an enviable ballast, a veritable kernel of strength. The workers arrived, rigidly encountering the days, watching them wash away in a floating procession. This observation stayed with me for months when I coursed to survey the mounting energies of rush-hour traffic, the outward bursts and eruptions of people everywhere. I felt a sadness inside that couldn't speak, to watch a population so lonely, and to feel myself, there, unnoticed.

When the train finally pulled into its destination for the first time, the hours closing in, the night falling like a blanket on the warm aftermath of the carriage, busied for another day and poised to retire, I'd take a moment to imbibe the silence and mystery left behind. Amid the discarded piles of rubbish and half-mounted table rests, a slow wind would wind its way busily across the seats, blending the faint body odours of the recently departed train passengers in a long concomitant stream. And time itself would appear so tenuous that it barely grazed me.

The temperature had dipped considerably by this time and yet something about the musty, fetid air suggested warmth and life even when the piercing cold tunnelled coarsely through.

The ride to the depot was never more than an adjunct to the day's events, events that I shall go on to discuss at greater length later on. Holing up beside other vehicles for the night, I watched the lights go out on the day and the journey, knowing that all I could do was wait for better times and be patient.

Despite the mostly gratifying wonder I found in navigating the train, I often suffered extreme outbreaks of tiredness and fatigue in unguarded moments of self. I wondered at times if my immersion in systems of such magnificent technological complexity could have had a less than benign influence on my memory. For often I was adept at feeling distressed or heavy hearted when I began to question the things around me.

If I pleased myself by observing how the train announcements rolled seamlessly across the electronic ticker tape with no noticeable errors, the systems dutifully in accordance, then I was equally fraught with worry on other occasions when my mind misted over and nothing made sense. Everything seemed full of both promise and menace, the future stretching out shakily before me.

When this dull, immaterial torpor overcame me, I'd often see a vision of threads laid alongside one another, borne up by many others, but resounding with so much noise that my whole being seemed to flicker tenuously like a flame on the edge of extinction. At times, I felt lost in a spiral of my own reckoning, strangely abstracted and yet, at the same time, plunged in a whirlpool of minute and contradictory deliberations.

My ideas were to some extent delimited by the train carriage, but they were frequently bent on issues extraneous to this setting, and more often than not, I found no answers to questions of fundamental importance. Considerations perked up as to the origin of my being; sequences of cause-and-effect stretching back centuries demanded explanation; everything considered true and unquestionable took on the aura of a seemingly ambiguous concept, constantly evolving and impossible to pin down.

Yet I was sure I had a right to withdraw from these delicate and complex situations and strove determinedly to avoid twisting myself in knots.

One time, when I looked out upon the

marshland, I was unsure whether the figures occupying the passing train were staring straight at me or directly past me, whether I was noticeable or if I was even there.

The nature of my presence was a continual concern to me, foregrounded, perhaps, more often than it should have been. And despite the intrigue I found in the stories I experienced on a mental level, I yearned for some kind of physical compensation to overcome my inadequacy.

Still, I gave no sizeable ground to these incursions, fending off the demons and retaining my strength. Again and again, my instinct brought me to my feet. Desperately, avidly, I would run for my life, and in the extremity I was revived and intoxicated by the irrational suffering and passion of the refusal to die.

With readily available shelter and stories beyond my means, it only fell to me to source nourishment for my time in the train carriage. Hunger would occasionally growl in my stomach like a pit bull and I'd scurry away to the storerooms where I could obtain sustenance adequate for my survival. I'd be able to wander past the guards without a care and gather the requisite articles without so much hassle.

Yet my nonchalance belied a certain emptiness, not only in terms of hunger but also when it came to the spirit, feeling full inside. Having till then been surrounded by figures of magnificent difference and variety, one event on an unbearably hot day caused me to reevaluate my situation. I found myself praising the simple pleasures thereafter, glad enough for the food in my belly as well as the sleep at night, when I lay to rest after the train had docked in the depot, wearing on my face a dream of a better tomorrow.

Often when passing through the pale expanse of the marshland, I would situate myself on the luggage racks overhead, perching on the cold, metal rails and drawing my legs up in a ball. This position attracted me most for reasons I only became aware of later on. It firstly offered unparalleled views of the countryside around the train, the carriage brightening up like a temple of space and light, the people within it saints in holy communion. I would see the marshes stretch that little bit further from here, inching their way ceaselessly towards the horizon, striving for the kind of release I so ardently fought for.

It fell upon me to decamp to this vantage point, secondly, as it seemed the aptest demonstration of my position in relation to the rest of the train passengers. When people talk of detached observation in an everyday social setting such as a dinner party, it rarely becomes them to understand the inherent isolation of any observation, the way that all human perspectives are by their very nature individual and limited.

The added solitude I'd been afforded by powers too big to understand - those same powers that would haunt my dreams at night with inescapable images of punishment and cruelty - deemed it appropriate that I be placed as an observer of a scene I could never truly become a part of. That coupled with the solace I received from the container-like space where I was holed-up, womb-like, in an area of manageable and circumscribed horizons, served to introduce this placating experience into my everyday routine.

One day, when the sun shone visibly against the frosty window panes, dissolving the glass in a translucent shimmer of inseparable crystals, a peculiar smell began to form in my nostrils. As the pungency of the odour increased, threading its way persuasively through the carriage and filtering up like an atomic cloud, a general air of panic seemed to take hold of the train passengers, causing many to leap up and shoot quizzical glances at one another.

I hadn't noticed such a display of energetic gesticulation before, the mood of the carriage, save the odd eruption, having mostly been placid and calm. Yet the brimming sense of tension and surprise was enough to flag up the discordance. It occurred to me how, when in the most comfortable and thoughtless environment, when one is breezily accepting of the unquestioned conditions and boundaries around them, the injection of some sort of challenge is enough to cause a quite alarming frenzy, our vulnerability showed up at its starkest, our survival instincts invigorated.

Almost immediately, however, and before a thought crossed my mind, I began to fear for my own self too, the anxious pack of dim, tormented faces brought together in a frightful and congealing mass. As separate beings merged into one, grabbing at one another's arms and clawing furiously, tremulous wisps of smoke appeared to form faces and an almost unbearable heat caught at the surface of my skin.

Barely aware of what had begun to take place in the carriage, I figured how the train passengers were now vacating the area, the train having stopped in its tracks. An announcement indicated the need to clear the vehicle, perhaps letting a little too much emotion into the voice.

No reason was given for this injunction, and the sense of urgency in the announcer's tone was unmistakeable. I was intrigued to discover the cause of all this alarm, but simultaneously helpless as I struggled vainly towards the door, unable to escape.

At the same time, I felt strangely guilty that I'd not been able to do more, cruelly helpless and pathetic. As the heat increased, my options became few, and the sensual pain I felt was an unwelcome reminder of my susceptibility to natural phenomena.

The announcer's voice struck panic in most of us, and I ran about as if possessed. Well-dressed men and ragged old women rushed around, shouting and entreating each other with vain pleas and concerns. Sparks began to fall into the carriage, eruptions emblazoned the window panes, and something that looked like fierce magic went shooting through the air.

There was nothing but smoke, fire and confusion, cries and curses, blows of splintering wood and slowly cracking glass. Within, the fire rumbled, crackled and gleamed.

A slow groaning sound turned into a rolling and a crashing and ended in a dull boom. Torturous flames gripped at those still trapped, pinching at dresses and coat tails, lapping away at the faces of the young, licking at the walls and windows. Jets of water that hissed and spluttered and splashed barely veiled the regular dull sob-like throb of the train's engine.

I wished ardently for at least a drop of cold, soothing water to fall upon me. But no one who passed by touched me – around there was nothing but air. Then the middle part of the ceiling started falling through into the huge, glowing chamber, pushing down and down.

I think I lost consciousness in a brilliant yellowish-white light, by turns unimaginably hot and thrillingly cold. In the midst of helpless moans and yelps, I felt my breathing stop.

As I look back at the time a fire broke out in the connecting chamber, still unenlightened as to its primary cause, its meaning or symbolic value, I begin to understand how hopelessly stranded we all are when we feel fear, how to accept yourself as you are, alone, discreet and vulnerable, is a necessary element of overcoming helpless abandonment to arbitrary and unreconcilable forces.

Yet the notion that to be free we must lose that sense of fear, lose that sensation of pain that reminds us that we exist, in this moment, in the here and now; this notion, I say, it scares me somewhat. In the same way that certain proponents argue for a brave new world without the human capacity to feel pain or sadness, hurt or suffering, through the implementation of new and flashy technology; the suggestion that human life would be hugely enriched by the negation of such an essential part of our nature disturbs me greatly.

Since the fire, I've consistently tried to improve my subliminal interaction with strangers, fending off the impulse of unreflecting fear when it naturally arrives. Watching people evacuate the carriage, I was keenly aware of my own inability to follow or escape the vehicle. But I still waited in trepidation as the masses gathered outside, unable to stay calm and reflect, caught up in the moment and swept along like a fish in a stream.

Feeling the power I possessed whipped from within me, I'd had my authority sapped, my superiority discredited. The fire had been unselective in its approach and stubborn in its goal, demonstrating the vulnerability of us all as it roared against the cold outside.

It is a reflection I carry with me now, through the days, coming no closer to a solution, nor despairing of my failure to consider it in the first place.

I wondered if I'd ever get to see the marshland but from a distance, for it continued to seem illusory and remote. I kept feeling like I was missing something or other when one morning, the dawn broke in a wash of pinkish light. I sensed a stronger connection to the marshland then, as if it were not simply the window-dressing to a scene, but somehow deep down within me.

Out of a brief period of mental block, when I felt quite dizzy and out of sorts, I stooped down to peer through the aisle and noticed the walls narrow and narrow. A great, piercing light emanated from the gap, the nucleus of an otherwise dark place. And the train seemed to huff and puff like a body, irresistibly beckoning me in.

My decision to approach was torn between an acute desire to get a hold of this nebulous aura spilling out from the adjacent carriage and an equally persistent urge to run away and seek cover.

At first, I felt quite nervous and anxious, my mind hurting a little at the inability to make sense of the situation or in any way evaluate the risk. Doing nothing was the safest option, but somehow this didn't seem acceptable.

I stared intently at the scene. The walls of the train carriage had detached themselves from the usual frame, casting off windows and overhead lights and anything that facilitated vision. They peeled away and flaked in a glassy, yellowish continuum, drifting towards some vaguely signposted point on the horizon.

Sight was obscured as the shadows became bluish bruises on the wallpaper, losing themselves in their own sparse ambiguity. Hushed, intimate expressions crept secretively from beyond the pale, and glass and metal clinked and scraped. The darkness seemed somehow to promise access to past days, days that formed from scattered flashes that disappeared back into the night.

None of my impressions rested with me though. Momentary inklings and darting intuitions crowded from every direction, each notion undermined by its own inherent dubiousness. Before I'd felt so secure, isolated as I was in my own little bubble. But as the space vanished, I was exposed like an infant to an unavoidable force, compelled to contend with a gaping blackness that enveloped me within its pages, likewise drawing me in and driving me away.

In the time it took to blink, the night had descended upon me, suggestive simultaneously of untold fears as well as a rather odd sense of comfort. Quite strangely, any anxiety had to contend with a sense deep down that now the darkness had come, we were unavoidably approaching the end of the day, nearing that final rest and release. My fear had been temporarily disposed of because I'd fought it, and not for the first time.

On numerous occasions in the train carriage, I'd have this extraordinary feeling of freedom when the sun finally set, discharging its duty to keep everyone awake and aware, pulling a veil over its scorching brightness, its endless efforts.

With the coming of the evening and nightfall, one senses that one's work is done for the day; that any further claims upon one's time can be met with less severity, less demand. That because we are no longer under the scrutiny of the sun's watchful and energising eye, we are free to take longer over our decisions, to be calmer in our interaction, to be more jovial and mild.

Rather than pressuring one into action, knowing that the end of the day is near seems to have the opposite effect in me of encouraging restfulness, as if sleep's universal grasp resides irrevocably within us all.

As reality lost its familiar outlines, gradually oozing away, I began to envisage the simple interactions and joys of a dinner party.

The meal was hosted in what looked like an ancient dining cart - the kind you no longer find, save in the passages of certain types of literature, appearing as if by rote in revered and time-honored texts.

No longer the hustle and bustle of the rush-hour traffic or the brusque arrivals and departures of the hurried train passengers; rather, time seemed to have been suspended temporarily, as if in remembrance of things past.

It was perhaps an outstanding symptom of my fall during the fire, but everything struck me choppy and disconnected like a dream. Some people appeared to be acting out pre-defined roles, assuming nonchalant airs, duly spouting received wisdom. I was unsure what this vision was meant to demonstrate. It was quite different to what I'd experienced before - both more real and more lived.

In traipsing across mountain tops or musing at the sides of train stations, I'd had access to alternative universes, other minds and thoughts. Never once, however, had I been plunged into a scene of such enveloping immediacy. I was no longer the observer, but somehow the protagonist of an event that struck me as oddly familiar.

All I could do to begin with was to

recognise that some experience was revealing itself to me, an experience heavily cloaked in the dusty half-light of lost time.

Soft voices drifted up through the fug of cigar smoke and flashing, clinking glasses heralded the beginning of a new course. Hearty laughter spilt fluidly from the ends of the table, piquing guests into action, emblazoning smiles and vanished gestures across the room. Gently coruscating music filtered through the carriage, filling up the empty passages and wordless lulls with universal breaths of life.

In savouring these opening moments I felt my body regress somewhat, my mind striving to recover something beyond its reach.

As I blinked hazily once more, I felt oddly ensnared, much like a wild animal caught in a trap. A group of floating figures approached me, patches of motion and uncertain voices springing up and passing away. The faces of the dinner guests arched round to meet me with inquisitive stares; stares that were kindly and plaintive; stares that refrained from the urge to put me on the spot.

As I stood there powerless and docile, they seemed willing to welcome a new face, a fresh onlooker. For a moment I saw myself as a child, standing nervously in loosely fitting clothes, clutching a glass of cloudy liquid that chilled my hands - not because it was full, but because

I felt so cold in my icy starkness.

A flutter of expectant excitement coiled around inside me as I moderated my slow, unapparent breathing. It felt like I'd been granted a moment of happiness that could relieve, if only for a few minutes, the consciousness of suffering. That period of youth, free from nauseating angst, free from the fear of change, tried to come back to me. But the words I spoke were uncertain and cannot possibly have cohered.

I don't remember them as I look back now, lost as they are in the breathy and spirited response of the kind lady who answered me. Her gently worn face and protective features transported me away helplessly in a cradled embrace. Her bronze hair shimmered against the dining lamp, centrally placed above the whole party. I wished to share in their affairs with intensity, to grow old and take part in them, instead of only being there as an onlooker. The lady drew the energies of everyone through her, gracefully caressing the air. She seemed to warm the whole room as she displayed her hand in a radiant sweep, drawing the sun out from within me.

In another moment, I saw myself wandering casually around the table, free to perceive others dispassionately, enjoying a strange and not unwelcome sense of knowing.

The guests were each ensconced in their own immediate surroundings and less concerned by visitors as by their particular meals. Yet I began unconsciously mimicking the behaviour of the individuals around the table, changing my persona to meet the needs of differing personalities and humours.

Still, the same lady remained though, a choreographed wave of her fan symbolic of the confidence and serenity she commanded over others. As she flicked her exotically patterned instrument back and forth, a fragrance composed of all the scents the world could contain wrapped itself around me, causing my heart to bound. She morphed effortlessly between roles: hostess, actress, seducer – inhabiting each one with complete assurance.

Yet this time, things were different. Perhaps I'd missed it before, but in her eyes I sensed something akin to the blackness of sin. It was all mixed up for me with the perfume. A kind of demonic charge escaped from her as if set free for the first time, released from a world of infinite possibilities and nauseous chance. Spilling out across the room, I felt myself vanishing under the weight of its force.

At that moment, I felt strangely warm and spiritual, as if the whole world was within me. Indeed, never had I been so fully lost in another person as to forget myself completely.

As my eyelids flickered, and utterly against my will, I heard my name being called, lightly, insistently. Before long, I found myself dropping into sightless, unconscious sleep.

"I've never been one to stare at things for too long; it makes my eyes hurt. I like to be constantly moving, always beginning afresh. If I think too much, I lose my time: it's stolen forever. So I bound along on my way, swinging a lantern in the castle maze, not minding so much about the others or what they think.

The clocks had stopped that night and time didn't seem to matter. There were people gathered around to celebrate the New Year but we could easily escape. Fire torches and streamers filled up the night sky, along with the yelps and cries of other children who could contemplate no better joy. The best times were when we crouched below a low-slung tree, hiding among the human-shaped fruit, but visible to no one.

It felt cosy and snug despite the cold. We toyed with the hanging ornaments in our little grotto, seeing how far we could push them before we caught someone's attention.

The danger nagged from a distance, but it was suitably remote to enliven as much as alarm. Outside our enclosure, the castle grounds were illuminated and I remember distinctly how a beam of light would occasionally flare up against the face of a passer-by, investing them with a temporary magic that vanished like the high-pitched scream of bats overhead.

The castle itself was manically grey, cast solid against the night sky, erected like a funeral. Behind its walls, it retained a little of the darkness of the night.

While we huddled there, joined occasionally by the odd wisp of green mist but nothing else, she asked me to hold her hand. I hesitated at first and wondered if it was a trick, thinking she'd perhaps scratch me. She said how it was good luck to hold someone when sitting beneath a tree. I remarked that I'd never heard of such a thing and she accused me of being too sceptical, of not having the necessary go.

That I had been too cautious was never a consideration that weighed too heavily upon me.

'Do you believe a word I'm saying?' she said, looking at me with the kind of reproachful face you'd expect from a parent.

'Why, am I not as faithful as a mirror? Can I not tell you the whole truth as you should see it?'

I must have looked somewhat puzzled as I sat there, bereft of a suitable response. My fingers feebly played with the pine needles that one by one dropped to the ground. She sounded like she'd whipped those words from a nursery rhyme or a fairy tale. Her eyes stared at me beadily like berries. I didn't like her tone and so scowled at her invitingly.

'My, you are an inquisitive type', she cried.

'Why do you want to know so much anyway? If you haven't heard of that, you're not going to hear of anything else with that attitude.'

With that curt retort, she darted off from under the tree, dragging her lantern with her and humming thoughtlessly.

She had a quite charming way of cocking her head, framed by the beautiful black picture of the sky. I'd look on in awe at her passion, seeing her as some kind of god or devil or something.

She whispered unremitting demands, something original in every breath, an exacting presence. She drew new strengths from her lips, her blood boiling like something wondrous, pulsing and tearing apart. But she made me feel cowardly and poor, an empty husk with emotion spent, my mind simply not capable.

'I'll lap you up with my tongue and let you swim there', she hollered, dancing indefatigably in circular motion.

'I'll nestle on your knee like a kitten and never leave'.

As I sat there, needling the grass, she kept taunting and goading me like some prolific minx. I became more enamoured and infuriated with her by the minute. Somehow she thought little, but through a profound intuition, always managed to settle on the right thing. Standing there in the moonlight she stood captured, as exquisite and timeless as a photograph.

I needed to feel all the tenderness that she inspired in me to react. But my vision had been ruined; we simply couldn't agree. I had nothing to give, nothing to show that could compare to her vitality. I sat there forlorn, pathetic and hopeless, wishing away the time I had to suffer, praying for relief.

Can a lifetime be judged on the back of one action? I couldn't leave it much longer. My imagination had forsaken me and my mind had locked up. Sheer panic had become me. I couldn't place her, so I ran away. But she had to be with someone from an early age, suffering as she did from a rare condition of the heart that meant she couldn't be left alone.

I always tore at her with questions, battled her with doubt. As I sprinted off, I was spurred to reflect on my actions, but my anger and shame were too much. As if I myself had done something to rouse the girl's fury, I asked, why should I be forced to put up with such larks? Why constantly made to feel so unsure? I seemed to constantly hunger for answers aside from the endless dilemmas she posed. Even if it meant failing the test, I simply had to leave.

As I staggered off out of the maze, I began to reflect on my existence as I'd known it. A life of spotless mediocrity, a touching and anxious devotion to life's little habits and tasks, a dull living of torpor and withdrawal: all made me utterly distraught. I was just too set in my ways.

And yet those same ways were me; they offered me comfort and solace to meet the day and face up to little minxes like her. Without them, I'd say, do you see what I'm like now? You think too much, she'd say. I'd run away once more.

She was taken to hospital the following day, my dreams of future happiness crushed like a plum underfoot. I was told that I could never see her again, let alone meet her in another's presence. She would remain a distant memory, a figure of unearthly rumination in my mind's eye.

I would return to that spot at the castle in a few years time, mournfully considering what could have been, certain that, given a second chance, I could have carried myself better."

I felt like I'd woken up as the scene crumbled away, but I couldn't be sure. I found myself suspended in a kind of well — teasingly deep and outside the train carriage - watching myself quizzically as I looked down.

Unaware of how I'd come to be there, a strange feeling of fear and longing overcame me. As I was transported above, thrown upwards as if turned inside out, I was able to look around at the landscape up close.

A distant region that I felt had once been near and in the present disappeared in a gulf before me. It seemed like I was walking across a supine body, a human, spongy floor that merged expertly with the earth. Erratic bursts of liquid shot up from crystal pools, mingling with other undefined ripples, becoming other, and other still. The sky was streaked through with a blitz of intermeshing lines that cut the night in a deep crimson glare. Forests that had once been barren and bare grew with great speed and motion, shrinking time to absorb the centuries. And as the wind blew harder and harder overhead, everything seemed tantalisingly poised, the threat of annihilation looming.

I was finally outside the train carriage, amazed by how familiar it all was, how much like an old home. I sensed that memories were slowly shedding their skin, peering up from the depths and combining in a glutinous swirl where neither the beginning nor end was visible.

I hadn't understood what had happened moments earlier and was certain that if I had, I could have made progress. But if scattered nostalgic flashes of happy days came to me, when they had passed the darkness was twice as black. If I was reaching hard to understand my roots, I was perhaps learning once more. But the wind tortured my skin as I stood out there, alone on the stricken marshland with nothing around for comfort except the thought that escape was possible.

Having been for so long in desperate awe of flight, in ardent and protracted longing for release from confinement, I'd now been plunged headlong into the world outside, removed from civilisation, exposed. The smell of the country was attractive and enlivening, the marshland retained a clear and harsh allure, and I was sure to recover from the rut I'd been in. But as long as I'd stayed between those train walls, I'd been able to fix the limits of probability. Today, they no longer fixed anything at all. I struggled to straighten my body, no longer propelled by the forward force of the train. Caught there in brutal apartness, I took a moment to acclimatise to the realisation of where I actually was.

The outside was something to be pitted against, something to be fought for survival. I tried desperately to concentrate, but my face seemed vague and fuzzy as the cold bore a hole in my cheek. I felt like some puddle stranded on a hill, unable to return to the sea.

I wondered with sudden panic if I was ever to go home to the train carriage, caught as I was and unable to go back. Neither seed time nor harvest was known on the marshes; everything seemed temporarily postponed.

Yet I sensed, simultaneously, a kind of burgeoning adventure, an opportunity for untrammelled and enlightened discovery away from sleep. I felt that, even if I hadn't found the thing I was looking for, the thing I was obsessed with, I'd still stumbled upon something else, something I'd absorbed somehow without quite knowing. Indeed, on several occasions thereafter, I heard within a soft, gentle voice which reminded me quietly, celebrating so that I could hardly hear it.

The air spoke of change, as brittle and

relentless as rain. The water ran brown and busy, sharp with its own purity, uncontaminated and without history. I shivered in the furious breeze and my eyes tightened to escape the ferment. From all around the wind keened and blew – a maelstrom of noise enveloping all. The fog accumulated quickly and I thought it wise to keep close to the side of the train, to hug it closely in case of squalls. But behind me the tracks were barren and no train was to be seen. Out of the fog, I began envisaging an assembly of houses, a symphony in grey securely knitted to the hillside.

I stumbled determinedly across some rocky outcrops towards my goal, the ground crackling under foot like a frosty fire. My shoes were dripping with dew and the rushes were almost too thick to walk through. But I was spurred onward by the prospect of human interaction.

As I approached the township, I noticed how tightly coordinated the urban milieu was. It wasn't merely that the apartments, office blocks, and warehouses were constructed in uniformly patterned grids, spaced homogeneously and administered with a rigidly even hand; nor was it the fact that each group of structures was confined to a designated and specific location on the terrain. No, rather it was the fact that every apartment was made up of regular cells of equal height, width and length; that every office comprised identical columns of rectangular blocks; that each warehouse was formed from exactly the same logical fashioning of bricks into straight, vertiginous walls.

The space had been unflaggingly systematised, conceived as a pattern that had then been filled in with greater and greater regularity over time. Rectangular houses formed rows, then streets, then blocks. Signs repeated themselves at identical intervals along the roads, framing each journey with impossible similarity. And maps were written into the town's texture, making navigation a seamless, static enterprise. Out on the perimeter, the shrub bushes shrugged indolently, each hardy leaf a perpetual slave to the elements.

I wandered on, my feet swept up speedily by a concrete path that appeared as if from nowhere. My first instinct was to question the location of the township, built so conspicuously as it was on hazardous terrain. Flooding was a perpetual threat on the marshland, and a thin film of water would accumulate in no time, supporting countless seabirds and migrating fowl.

The weather would change rapidly as

well. Winds would careen across the flats, wholly oblivious to human measures of defence. It perplexed me how the citizens of this strangely isolated place had succeeded in establishing themselves in the first place. Clearly, stringent plans had been enacted to coordinate and consolidate the construction. Perhaps this was the only way to manage such a mammoth task of mathematically parcelling out the infinite.

Still, something of the futility of the enterprise struck me, the way everything had to have its place, the way things were only ever either or.

Large, whitewashed walls formed the outer perimeter of the town. Within this space, a fixed network of courtyards, churches, and administrative and workers' quarters spread out silently.

The grid itself seemed an awesome expression of a highly regulated, tightly administered culture. Buildings had been made to remove all signs of defects or contamination. Different districts were codified and housed to support the various needs of the population. And food was evidently sourced from the granaries that, in number, directly reflected the city's estimated population.

Located within the larger residences

inhabited by wealthy officials in the north, the granaries were oddly distanced from everything else. Indeed, there appeared a curious antagonism between the two habitations, as if no serious attempt had been made to integrate the different peoples or to cope with social and economic differentials.

Wandering past the first of the outlying houses, I chanced to look in upon the make-up of a school. Identical desks were arranged in rigidly set-about grids; screens and ledgers lay propped up against the sideboards; and metal quadrants hung from the walls. No activity took place inside, however, the day perhaps being a weekend.

The moon had risen over the still waves on the horizon and the sea was momentarily indistinguishable from the sky. As I trundled on, I coursed upon a solitary gas lamp, peculiar and isolated afar, appearing as some lighthouse at the edge of the world.

Shining half-obscurely from inside a remote dwelling, the light merged with a pungent smell filtering up from the blackish sludge underfoot to lend a remarkable impression to the scene. Indeed, I was distinctly troubled by how this particular house had, for one reason or another, been abandoned as part of the urban environment, how the harsh coherency of the cityscape had been allowed to slip. The dwelling itself was shaped like a wigwam, its walls arching toward a pointed horizon. Strange blocks of colour made up the sides and a wooden ladder offered the opportunity to climb to a balcony with a better view.

My footsteps disappeared in the scarcely perceptible distance as I sought refuge before the maw of darkness. Wandering furtively around the side of the house, I was also eager to escape the fast brewing storm. Raindrops had begun exploding in momentary bouncing fountains that turned into bubbles and burst. A haze rose off the brown marshes as though the ground itself were rising to meet the scooping sky. As the rain streamed wantonly, the reflected heavens were full of tiny dancers, water fairies springing up on edge like bright pins rising from the surface.

As I peeled away from the pathway, I noticed a rapidly emerging pool of light spill out across the floor, enlarging and celebrating the building, blending the moistened tufts of grass into the shadows.

The moon had taken on a distinctly brighter hue as the rain cleared, dappling the cinder-strewn patches of grass and piles of slate-coloured rubble with indefinite shimmers. I considered with a mixture of excitement and fear the prospect of finally finding someone to talk to. Armed with questions and dilemmas that pierced to the root of my existence, I felt like a man on a mission. But I struggled to locate an opening to the house and no windows or panes existed to signal the coming of visitors.

I wondered for a moment how I'd been able to locate the building in the first place, for there was no clearly defined plot and the wooden walls resembled barely finished structures, shimmering like vaporous imaginings.

As I stood there, frigid and stark, the thought that I may not find the elixir I was hoping for began to trouble me, suspended like an immovable shadow in the cage of my heart.

It occurred to me then, after a brief consideration of the facts, that I'd failed to notice the lamp this second time because of the unique direction from which I'd approached the house. Coming from the town, I learned, one would only ever perceive the rear of the building, thus denying a view of the tenement's full perspective.

I must have fallen off course to begin with, stumbling from the usual, established path, and been offered an uncommon outlook not normally granted others. From where I stood now, the house had an unparalleled prospect on the plains; something akin, I figured, to the pioneer spirit of yesteryear.

I really had no idea of what to expect from the house, who to envisage answering the door, the kind of response I was likely to receive.

As I stood there, hunched over in the bitter chill, I felt sour at being made to undergo this penance. Gazing at the passing clouds, I was vacant, childlike before the restless wind. My mind felt drowsy, pulled away by the distant tide. My eyes sore and frosty.

All of a sudden, I began to notice a coat of arms adjacent to the door-handle, appearing as if in relief. I couldn't make out the exact design of the object, for it was veiled somewhat by the inclement weather. Yet I reckoned it resembled something like a petalled flower in white upon a black background. Underneath the symbol were several lines of indecipherable lettering in a language I couldn't make out.

Before I could look any longer, the door to the house was wrested open. A prim looking lady, dressed entirely in grey, and possessing a face dour enough to match the extremity of the night, met my stare. She glared at me with a querulous, querying gaze, indicating the depth of her intentions. Her pale, almost ghost-like eyes were framed by a series of wrinkles that dissolved the cold outline of her face, extending like ripples or branches or wasted laughter lines. And her hair was tied back in a bun, shackled from the tense, frosty armour of her neck.

I have never been one to force my way or cause undue alarm, but I found myself instinctively darting a foot at the door as the lady pressed it shut. Through some freak accident, however, the door slammed in front of me, and the words nobody there rang out from beyond the threshold.

I figured that I'd have to find some other form of access to the building if it were ever to be disclosed to me what lay inside. My tickling fear at encountering another human being had been usurped by the painful realisation that I would remain unseen. This impression was moderated only for an instant as I reflected on the cold and accusative stare I'd just received. Before long, I experienced the irresistible grab of curiosity, urging me to go on.

A mighty gust of wind ripped past me, an unexpected reminder of the outside world. To my good fortune, the door to the house was shoved ajar, released from its unsteady latch. The dimly lit room spread out before me, emanating a faint orange glow. In a panic to examine my surroundings, to soak up all available impressions before the opportunity lapsed, I hurriedly cast my eyes this way and that.

The room was of a modest size, unassuming in its dimensions and strangely enclosed in a way that appeared both furtive and cosy. The walls were adorned with numerous maps, town plans and grids packed with curious, latent meaning. The ceiling seemed to sink in, patchy with wet blotches, bowing under the drooping pressure of animal hides, tanned and dressed. Across the floor lay scattered remnants of straw, yellow strands full of smokey dampness.

As I experienced that warm, safe feeling of escaping inside after rain, several people appeared before me. The lady – already mentioned – with a dour, pale complexion; a man – perhaps the husband – equally morose and stern; and a younger child, sitting patiently and inquisitively on a wooden stool.

I stepped inside the dwelling, not expecting to draw any notice upon myself, unperturbed by my assumed role as unseen interloper. The stares of the occupants turned to focus on me.

"I thought I told you to see to that door, Marjorie. It's not like I don't have enough on my plate as it is."

The man in the large, grey overcoat broke the bristling silence with strict, peremptory words. Across the room, the lady bent her head towards the floor, returning to a sideboard that demanded her attention.

The whole impression for me was one of becoming. The dim light perhaps made this more noticeable than it would otherwise have been. The man's words hovered about the room disagreeably. They could have been met with a number of responses, but none were decided upon.

"It's common sense. I've told you what to do before. Why can't you follow simple instructions?"

As if the man feared that his words may go to waste, he tore about the room, stomping heavily. He seemed unable to stand still, the prim lady a surface across which his outbursts could stream.

"We can't have so many little things outstanding, Marjorie. You must understand that we must be ready at any time."

The man spoke assertively, hungering for control. I wandered towards one of the sideboards and chanced upon a series of instruction manuals and carefully collated plans. A quick study of the documents demonstrated an unmistakable likeness between the drawings and the town I'd recently departed. From the sketches, it appeared as though the town had been conceived to expand outwards, but that perhaps this objective had yet to come to full fruition. Either this or various untoward circumstances had prevented it from happening.

Yet there was something of a secretive air to the diagrams before me, as if they had been mislaid or misappropriated by unsuitable hands. The man's hurried aspect, his hastily exchanged words and anxiety that seeped out like a bad spirit, made me wonder about his role in the matter.

"Would you pass me those papers, Marjorie?" he exclaimed.

I took a step back.

"I haven't gone through it all yet," he grumbled defensively.

"I don't understand any of it," said the lady, breaking her silence with an unsteady confidence that ill became her.

"To me, it's just a blank sheet of paper."

"It's common sense, Marjorie," the man retorted, plainly unwilling to enquire further into the woman's ignorance.

He leafed through the papers with brusque determination, seeking to absorb all and sundry as if to package it up and put it away for good. He looked uncertain and undecided, and this seemed a direct cause of his disgruntlement. I myself felt uncomfortable and unable to relax around the man, finding myself drawn sympathetically to anyone who opposed him.

In an instant, the man looked up towards nothing in particular, his face beaming.

"That's it," he exclaimed, seeming to find solace in the answer he'd stumbled upon.

"I understand it now, I do. This is a great day, Marjorie, for I have discovered the plans, truly I have. The town will answer to me now."

The woman looked faintly pleased but hesitant to commit to a response. Her manner, in fact, was so cautious and provisional that it made her the object of little attention. She looked afraid as if she was constantly aware of what was coming.

Across the room, my sight was caught by the small child resting wraith-like on a stool. His placid, flickering eyes gazed directly at me as if he knew I was there, as if he possessed the solution to life's most mysterious secrets.

The boy was ensconced in a safe sheath of darkness, nestled away in the corner of the room as if he'd learned through experience to keep out of the way. He held a kind of tool - perhaps a chisel - that he prodded repeatedly at an intractable slab.

"You boy," came the hasty injunction from

the father.

"Come give your old man a hand will you."

The man said the words almost teasingly as if there were no reasonable hope of follow-up. The boy's eyes spoke of untrammelled optimism, a blindness to the notion of evil, hard labour, or anything contrary to love. Yet the older man betrayed an urge to push the boy, to harass him in a browbeating and inconsiderate way as if to see how far someone could degrade before they turned to nothingness.

"He'll stay here to help me work the land. He won't betray me, will you boy?"

The woman spoke up immediately.

"But he's too young to see to that kind of thing," she said, tears pushing through her cries.

"He should stay with me for another year, away from all that horror."

"Death, agh, it happens," said the man with an exaggerated shuffle.

"No hiding from it, I'm afraid."

The man seemed pleased in his opposition, breaking out in a welcome fit. His hard, proud heart had undoubtedly suffered much, and he enjoyed repeating certain lines as they afforded him a measure of certainty. His thoughts became his own, reinforcing his hidden conviction. In confirming his feelings and thoughts, he was given power and authority as an observer. To be sure, he was a hoarder, a secretive, restive man with plenty to prove.

"I've started this now, so we must finish. Boy, here."

As the man uttered those unkindly words, a curt outburst emanated from his lips.

"What is it dear?" inquired the woman, transformed instantaneously into the maternal and caring figure she always wanted to be.

"Just a little scratch," said the man, blood oozing from his hand.

"We must take you to the hospital, dear. You have hurt yourself."

"No!" came the response, brooking no argument.

"I cannot, and we must not. You must know that by now."

This dismissal seemed to have drawn an unimpeachable line under the issue, even though the blood continued to flow. With an undefined remorse and inner loneliness, I acquiesced, trying to see a way through with it. There was nothing I could do to intervene, and perhaps it wasn't my place. The man's stringent self-autonomy was not dissimilar to my own, and even if our worldly occupations were at odds, I made a concession for him, a kind of spiritual discretion.

Here was a man with life experience, I thought, who believed there was nothing new under the sun. He explained the new by the old, and the old by the older still. He had big gaps in his thinking, but by repeating things so many times, those around him absorbed his assertions like oxygen. I felt a sympathy then as if I would be like that one day.

I saw it as a challenge to myself, to not get angry, to remain composed. Perhaps my head was likewise buried in the sand. Perhaps I would commit the same follies. Maybe I would have to live through errors the like of which one cannot learn from except through living oneself.

I thought my time there nearly up when I motioned upon the woman once more, assuming the role of artist, her hands occupied with knitting needles and embroidery. She looked intensively at her work, a fleeting pleasure constantly under threat from inevitable change.

Beside her were a number of photographs, snapshots of moments that offered glimpses into a past I so eagerly wished to recover. That the images concealed as much as they revealed was hardly a surprise to me. Stripped of a broader context, the black and white photographs signified mere half-truths, morally, as well as visually. Resentful of anything but the immediate, perceptible locale, they were removed of all movement, sound, memories.

The camera's interruption of the flow of time is only illusory, I thought. People cannot go back or repeat. The desire to see what the world looks like in our absence is an impossible desire. I'd always be looking through the self-same eyes when I looked at anything. As I leant in closer, my sight was lost in shadow.

My last recollection is of walking out onto the swamp, a solitary feudal lord looking out upon a city of empty tombs. Unsure of what to make of the family that lived there, their relationship to neighbours – loved, if anything, only in the abstract - a slow procession of shapes coursed across the ground. All along the adjacent brick wall, concealed thumb marks housed chinks of grass, and a stream of smooth, babbling voices leapt against the mossy verge.

I knelt down to try and take hold of the river, but it ran away, forming puddles that never dried up. My claustrophobia returned, along with an irrepressible wave of sadness and I closed my eyes to sleep.

When I awoke, it was with a shadowy sense of fear that I imagined what I'd just seen to be something I'd known before as a child. Brooding, restless notions of something ever so slightly out of reach rankled inside. The train screeched in anger, throwing up a wall of sound around me. And I scraped my nails with displeasure across the carpeted, numb floor of the carriage.

Never before had I felt so urgently the need to recover the ability to see clearly; to rediscover that state of childhood wonder and grabbing after the infinite. To free myself from the blurry, irresolute shackles of my current idly reflective state, I was instinctively inclined to think more and more, to try and analyse and reason my way out of the mire. But in the same moment, I hungered for a kind of silence, an open space to sit back and savour, to let the memories come back on their own. For I felt that I hadn't been thinking, merely toying and that there were many stores of lost time reaching out for me.

I mused briefly. I simply couldn't see anything anymore. However much I searched the past, I could only retrieve scraps of images, and I was not sure what they represented, nor whether they were remembered or invented.

Whichever way I turned, I kept coming up against locked doors. If I wanted the moments of my life to become ordered, for the light to ward off the darkness, then across the marshland, the sun remained concealed behind shifting, spinning clouds, offering a token of brightness but nothing more. If I wanted my focus to narrow, to hone in on the immediate and be sure of itself, then my mind equally drifted outwards, toward the broader context, towards the random and chaotic.

I'd repeatedly had the urge while on the train to talk to someone, only to find myself staring for hours at the floor. I could address the light that shimmered like dust through the window or make conversation with the hillsides and their silently suspended verges. But I felt foolish and stupid in my self-enclosed ways, the desert vacancy of the marshland residing deep within me.

I was intensely irritated that I couldn't think and deeply wary of what I didn't understand. At the same time, I figured how I'd not been spending much time in the present, abstract speculation making up most of my waking moments. That this had compounded and reinforced the chronic sense of loneliness I'd felt day-to-day was never in doubt. In my apartness, I had yearned for a sense of order, a way to control things and clear my own head.

When I could have mingled, I had gone away; when I had something to share, I took it as my own.

Indeed, never had I felt so strongly as then that I was devoid of secret dimensions, limited to my body, to the airy, fleeting thoughts which floated up from it like bubbles. The opportunities that had been held out to me had been missed and I felt that somehow I'd had wonderful moments irrevocably taken away.

I passed reflection on myself for a moment. I consider myself guilty of pride. I am not unjust towards my fellow man; I endeavour to be just and patient towards them. But I have never loved them. The work, troubles, pleasures, and follies of others are more unknown and remote to me than the moon. Indeed, it is a wonder that my heart hasn't dried up completely. Amid the hellish blindness, perhaps a small spot remains within me that can be reached by grace.

I no longer thought I had a past life, but wanted to know how it would feel if I did. I'd grown sick of reflection, and thought it was about time I plunged myself straight in.

Since the time of the dinner party, half-finished words had roamed my mind, making them noisy and unresolved - making them appear to run away. The ebb and flow of consciousness had left me confused and without peace, my resolution tending toward inertia. My emotions, too, had undergone violent shifts - then happy, then sad, then noble then savage - forcing me to confront my own self in all its volatility.

I kicked out my legs with useless but unstudied aggression as I regained a footing, knowing somehow that I had to go on. My poise had taken on a more cautious gait, for I feared for which way I was to go.

Somewhat harshly, the train carriage assumed a kind of intense hostility where my footsteps sounded hollow, where everything was incomplete. Yet simultaneously, I no longer felt the need to course through the carriages like a madman, soaking up each step with the kind of cold, inhuman haste I'd taken before. While before the train had played the part of a kind of foil for me, it now seemed entirely arbitrary and fake, and I dreaded that I'd no longer be in a position to react should I chance to come across someone.

It struck me then that, on the one occasion when I had been outside the train carriage, I had only walked through the city one way; that I had navigated the space from a single, solitary direction. This recognition spurred the thought in me that the town contained a greater seed, the prospect of becoming a dense and lively forest of infinite possibilities.

That I had only experienced the outside from a single vantage point seemed to reflect on my experience in the train carriage as a whole. The fact that I had been restricted to a vehicle that travelled along the same tracks, back and forth like a shuttle, appeared highly revealing.

As I cast a glance around the train, we shot out through a dark tunnel, reappearing into the light, after rain. The sun beamed its sparkling rays against the side of the cliff, igniting tufts of grass that dotted the precipice in a breathless array of luscious greens and browns. The rooftops that blanketed the town absorbed the warmth and rain droplets shimmered in a humid haze. Inside the carriage, minute specks of white dust tumbled in slow flow through the glittering air. And all the while the train kept on its course, streaming past more and more people as they walked up and down the long, steaming streets.

For a distinct moment, the train appeared as if it were a part of the sky, its windows a giant portal to the atmosphere. Outside of my control, memories began fluttering up like fish, spawned through my body like salmon struggling upstream. All that chaos and disorder, I thought, all that sheer mess of the earliest moments rankled deep within me. But my instinct to contain and to measure, to conceptualise and to put away, was dimmed – it no longer amounted to the iron-clad dictum it had proved to be in each conceivable instance before.

All around me, things were moving. People shuffled and whispered, spaces shifted and transformed, the air spun and fluttered. Never for a moment were things still. The train was a solid, substantial thing that weft and weaved through the country and the city, to be sure. But beyond my line of vision – through a lens deeper and more elemental than that seen in the everyday - atoms and molecules flexed and fired in excited and irascible firestorms. Actions augured reactions and energy burst out of timid shells without ever coming to rest. The wind was a primal force to disturb and unsettle. But it also sped things on their way, carrying cycles to impossible ends, termini that recede endlessly into the mist.

Everything is changing, I thought, always, and nothing is so fixed as the frame we get used to seeing before our eyes.

The land around me had borne witness to this dizzying display of acrobatics, this fundamental play of the stars where nothing ever dies. The hills hadn't missed an inch, treating each new occurrence with the same impartial and unequivocal pretext. I myself had fallen into a typically human battle with disorder, a desire to see myself as a pivotal actor in a scene of my creation. I'd sorted events into manageable sequences, layered them with meaning and certainty, carved my life-story out of an unlikely introduction.

But the thing I held fashioned in my hands had begun to wilt, to dry out, suffer and perish. Its colour had waned, its milk had turned sour, and it sagged soundlessly like a still-born child. As the train rattled across the bridge, the almighty ocean began to tail us by the twice-stripped coast, reaching up in a lolling drift against my machinery.

I ran about hurriedly, eager to imbibe any tastes or smells that could revive a distant past. It appeared as one last chance, something I had to seize now or be forever left with regret. My heart grew heavy as I caught my breath. I thought I'd lost what little opportunity I'd had, my vision growing dim.

Out of the silence of the marshland, and behind a gently swaying curtain, there appeared a picture of a bustling market - a sight for sore eyes, of which I have often been reminded since.

I could only make out fragments of eyes

darting about restlessly, hands fondling goods, arms raised in energetic gesticulation. But the impressions I received spoke loudly to my solitude and I warmed to the activity like the sun on an early riser. From an unknown corner, someone was saying something, and I was sure it was directed at me. As I twisted around, miraculously thieving colours and sounds, the whole thing descended in a rush.

Everything was external, outside of full view and uncontained. But a vaporous figure, sheathed in overalls and lumbered with boxes and casks began spreading his arms.

Words poured from his mouth like the sea, lapping at my hardy shore.

"You are not your mind", he said, repeating it twice, a full, flowing sensation of something deeply intuited washing over me.

"Your thoughts are your own, and they come from you. Your stories are yours, and yours only."

The import of the man's words did not dawn on me right away, and I figured if they had, I may have been able to respond better. The whole notion appeared as something I should passively indulge, and the force of the man's words disarmed me like a steady breeze.

The figure pointed searchingly at the electronic display screen which flickered like an intermittent bulb above my head, revealing nothing but himself. I sensed then that my mind was playing tricks on me, but that what had passed between the strange market-seller and myself was in some way close to my heart.

Was he somehow saying that I had lived the duration of my time on the train carriage inside my own head? Was he insinuating that the stories I took as insights into my own past were conjured not from the abstract thoughts of my fellow passengers, but from the depths of my own distant memory and imagination? If this was so, it would explain how I had become less and less willing to accept interruptions on my carefully honed universe, how I had subsisted largely happy in the carriage, bothering absolutely no one.

What then was I to make of the significance of the visions I had had? Had I been all this while constructing my own life in what I determined to be my own image, dreaming all things so as to transform them into my substance? And had I no greater access to the thoughts and tribulations of others than anyone else?

Bounding myself in a limited horizon, latching on to familiar routines, I was my mind only, self-absorbed like my first traveller. Trapped in a terrible echo chamber of the self, a kind of nightmare of the soul, my ability didn't carry nearly the weight I'd supposed. Attracted to figures who mimicked or resembled me in some way, the experience I'd had had been alone, and it felt like no experience at all.

For other people were mere channels, fickle conduits through which a sea of thoughts flowed according to my own fancy. And as I loved what was solid and formed, not what was becoming and insecure, I couldn't escape myself, the taste becoming all-consuming and more distinctive than anything.

And what of the patterns I had intuited. I knew they existed, to be sure, but they were not the ones I had found, and I was no closer to knowing where I had come from than when I'd started. A strong feeling of awakening from a long lethargy, a sense of distress slipping off came over me. And I walked on again like a man who knew what he had to do.

Indeed, that was a memorable day for me, for it initiated great changes. But it is the same with any life. The constraining nature of classification prevents one from making new discoveries, and it renders thinking stagnant. My existence free of clutter had served a purpose, but its desirability was now questioned against an alternative vision of chaos and mess. My self-imposed illusion had been vital for my happiness. But my inability to understand this illusion as just that meant I'd stored up disappointment for years to come, and I now felt powerless to stop the storm as it poured down on me.

My mind had tried to wrap itself around the world like a glove, but it had left no room for the fingers or toes, nor for the bristly hairs that poke out through the fabric. I had thought that knowledge would grant me happiness but my notion of total understanding was an impossible dream.

In fact, I was wrong - I was not free and my existence had been a lie. My need to understand had been the root of my problem and it had led to a kind of false unity, imposed and unchecked. Indeed, never before had I understood so clearly how the world doesn't obey fixed and unchangeable laws; how easily constancy can vanish; how it is gone in a breath.

Everything is contingent, and you can never ultimately deduce anything, I thought. There are people, I believe, who understand this. There are people who have tried to overcome this contingency by inventing a necessary, causal explanation. But no necessary being can explain existence.

Like a weathered cork bobbing on a crest of sea, the tempestuous currents of life crossing in endless cycles, we stay afloat, grasping at that intangible, negative space atop the fathomless ocean. And we manage to muddle on, even if a sense of progress, a sense of forward motion without instant relapse, is never free from doubt.

The passage of time becoming imperceptible, save for the sudden interruption of an aggressive eddy or the unanticipated eruption of a whirling plume, the waves brush past us continually, awaiting, with impregnable indifference, that final, summative breath.

I had grown older; I was weary and solemn. A cold figure who'd experienced neither success nor failure, my voice had become hesitant, and my hope had waned. As for routine, I cannot think of such things now. I simply don't want to know. The man in the brown overcoat who I'd met with those weak, colourless eyes, that closed-down, torpid mind, was me.

So, why the train carriage in the first place? For what reason was I sent here? And was there even a reason at all? These questions of meaning became most prominent in the ensuing hours, minutes, moments; foregrounded like a sharp frost, icily nipping at my fingers and toes. I was on edge to discover, tense with eager fright. I felt all of a sudden removed from my surroundings, on the brink of a new knowledge, alien yet all-knowing. And yet I knew now how my superiority and mastery had been stripped like so much bark from a tree. Bare as a twig, brittle as the autumn leaf, uprooted by a force of wind unimaginable and uncaring, who was I now and where was I to go? Would that there were something somewhere that could retrieve me from this madness!

The questions were as meaningless as they were ill-posed. Something had brought me here as penance, a kind of retribution for a life misspent. And I had a suspicion that the kinds of dilemmas I was fronting myself with were exactly of the kind that had landed me here in the first place. I felt guilty, guilty for being unable to do things. The practical things, the basic things, these eluded me and I knew the web of guilt and uncertainty I wove around myself had separated me in a crucial way from my fellow man. I was constantly apt to categorise, exhaust and explain, and this flood of imposing order meant I withdrew, seeking everything, doing nothing. For as long as I can remember in the train carriage if not before, I had been painfully aware of every word and its meaning. I'd retreated to a hinterland of the soul, and this had become my ordained refuge.

Would that I could change! Would that this was the reason I had been sent here; that I could shake this condition off like so much damp stuff drying on the line. Yet how was I to know what was on the other side, what fate would befall me were I to leave this closeted realm, a realm I'd grown fond of in all my apparent fear and trepidation? Was I right to look further into myself now I'd been shown the fallacy of my whole experience on the train carriage? Had I been truly false anyway, and how was I to know what was and wasn't me?

Is this questioning guilt a disposition of my nature, an unalterable facet of my temperament, or has it been nurtured in me by repeated experience, by the forces of a society governed by particular values and the time-specific attitudes of those closest to me? Has this proclivity, this flaw, been fostered and absorbed internally among sets of ancestors, transmitted from generation to generation, and now so wholly ingrained that it has become, by all accounts, inescapable? Is my guilt symptomatic of an unjustifiably exalted view of the significance I play in the world? Or could it be the transference of all the sin ever dealt by humanity upon the head of one individual, aware of his moral responsibility and the contingency of his behaviour?

I figured it was useless to keep posing

these questions, of all the places I was. I was more and more resembling a morbid personality, the antithesis of the bright, intrepid soul I'd been while under the illusion of omniscience. If I was more in line with the unflagging movement and brimming change of the train carriage when I was deluded, won over to my own importance and sense of purpose, then I now resembled a discarded heap, a slag pile left to mould and fester by the side of the track, so static and motionless for being weighed down by so much. I was obsessive, paralysed, caught up so inextricably in my own self, a tight ball of conflicting and uncontrollable chemical energies while everything around me was expanding, moving effortlessly along. If I wanted to keep up, to live and to move, I had to drop the agonising questions, the fear that was a psychological barrier to everything I was, everything I could ever be. I would deny my former self, the wasted, self-interested not me, and attain a newer, fresher reality. I would learn to laugh and accept this strange physiology, this science, this humanity. My vital memory of this, I thought, may have passed with all the rest.

I looked out across the frost-littered marshes and snow had begun to fall. The sky looked alive but unthreatening, a blushed kind of grey turning to brilliant white. I let my anxiety drop as surely as the flakes hit the ground. My eyes shone back at me in the reflective glass, as big and bright as stars. I repeated to myself because I thought I'd heard it somewhere before: may the days be aimless, let the seasons drift, do not advance the action according to a plan.

I felt then that I could do anything, but that at the same time I may not want to, that my keenness may float away in a pool of quiet calm. I felt the eyes of my fellow train passengers press up against the glass too, a force of motion so strong as to shatter anything in its path. We watched as the waters rolled and the grasses swelled; we watched the sky as it turned over 180 degrees; we watched the sun occupy the sky with beaming munificence, hidden modestly behind a wash of fluffy white clouds; and we watched as the earth changed, and we changed too.

A huge roar emitted from behind me as if something had spun out of control. The man in the brown overcoat rested his hand on the seat beside him, as if to replace someone gone away. The snow had begun falling more heavily now, the floor a blanket of packed ice, a strange blurring of land and water. What a wonderful story I thought, the best there was. Not an unattainable story, the kind you tell yourself to portray an ideal. Rather, a true story, a story of the elements, of hot and cold, pleasure and pain, of this moment, of now.

Each snowflake fell, different in its own remarkable way. I felt myself pushing against the door of the train carriage. This time, with the slightest effort, it gave way.

I could have been left for hours in that state, for days. In fact, I probably was. My mind had kept me there, desperately securing its own image of perfection. But like a plant that has to shed its outer layer before coming to full bloom, I was finally seeing new shoots, shoots that weren't perfect - how could they ever be? - but shoots nonetheless, shoots of a magisterial beauty as lovely as the sunset or the breeze. And there I was, as alert as I'd ever been, close enough to see myself again, a lover, a wanderer, with all my baggage in tow.

I took in my hand those of the other passengers as we all ran out into the sun. On my one side, the man in the brown overcoat, his thoughts as empty as mine, his face lit up. On my other, the fading spectacle of the train carriage, a shadowy body of pitch black, a pool of darkness, the irresistible light pouring in. We were running; from what I cannot say. All I knew was that there was nothing we needed to run from, but that we must, for all our sakes.

My calm is made of quiet resignation. I'm always learning, awaiting with deep humility and patience the birth-hour of a new clarity.

One final thought: of walking into a warm room, the door open, my pulse beating.

———————

Acknowledgements

My designer and long-term friend Thom Burgess.

Keith and Karolina at Michael Terence Publishing for being so supportive and agreeing to publish my first novel.

Friends and family from Whitstable, London and Canterbury.

My parents Lizanne and Andy, my sister Emily, my family.

My grandmother Mary. This book is for you.

Those no longer with us.

Those with whom we've spent loving moments but with whom we won't again.

Lads and lasses I know from Simon Langton School, still friends after all these years.

The staff at Lewisham University Hospital and South London and Maudsley NHS Trust who helped me through a recent crisis. Long live the NHS.

Francine.

Staff and students at Goldsmiths University from 2006 to 2009, many of my ideas come from being with you.

Leslie Tate and Susan Hampton, writing buddies.

Eleanor Heidingsfeld, get well soon.

Everyone at ATD Fourth World in Camberwell and elsewhere.

Malpas Road crew, Brockley.

Friars Close.

The Tea and Times. The Fountain - you're still going!

My good friend Kenji.

Max Lucas aka Mime aka Max Skillz aka legend.

Rita, wherever you are.

Alex Leone, well done mate.

Southeastern trains, for better or worse.

The marshes between Whitstable and Faversham, which form the bedrock of this book.

Train travel in general, long may it continue.

The Guardian newspaper, still my go-to news source and the inspiration for several episodes in this story.

Travelling.

Music.

South-east London.

The far north of Scotland and the British landscape in general.

Building(s) in Stone, the book's original working title.

Anyone else I've not mentioned, with you in spirit.

Matthew Allcock was born in Canterbury in 1986. He has lived most of his adult life in Whitstable, Kent where he grew up and in London, where he is now based, and where he studied English at Goldsmiths.

At university, Matthew achieved the highest mark in his year. A writer of literary prose and poetry for several years, Matthew was long-listed for the Cinnamon Debut Poetry Collection Prize in 2012 and for the Cardiff Review Short Story Award in 2016.

His short stories and poems have been published widely in online zines and blogs including the London Journal of Fiction and Jotters Utd. Matthew has travelled extensively, namely to China where he taught English for two years.

Matthew makes music under the name Lipsis, and already has three albums released.

The Man on the Train is his first published novel.

Available worldwide from

Amazon

_____

author@matthewallcock.com

_____

www.matthewallcock.com